A Split in Time

How to Write Dual Timeline, Split Time, and Time-Slip Fiction

MELANIE DOBSON &
MORGAN TARPLEY SMITH

A SPLIT IN TIME

HOW TO WRITE DUAL TIMELINE, SPLIT TIME, AND TIME-SLIP FICTION

MELANIE DOBSON

MORGAN TARPLEY SMITH

INK MAP PRESS

A SPLIT IN TIME

For more information, address inkmappress@gmail.com.

Published in Pollock, Louisiana, by Ink Map Press

www.inkmappress.com

Cover Design by Victoria Davis

Cover Image (left): Stokkete/Shutterstock

Cover Image (right): Leszek Czerwonka/Shutterstock

Library of Congress Cataloging-in-Publication Data

by Dobson, Melanie and Smith, Morgan Tarpley— 1st edition

A Split in Time / how to write dual timeline, split time, and time-slip fiction
LCCN 2020910613
ISBN 978-1-952928-02-4 (trade paper)
ISBN 978-1-952928-03-1 (ebook)

1. Writing Skills 2. Composition & Creative Writing

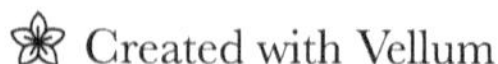 Created with Vellum

Melanie's Dedication

Natasha Kern
For Encouraging Me to Dream

Morgan's Dedication

Carole Lehr Johnson
For Friendship and Faith

Table of Contents

"A Split in Time is the only craft book I know devoted completely to writers who want to write in the time-slip genre. With skill born of experience, Melanie Dobson and Morgan Tarpley Smith explore everything from the perks split time fiction offers to practical ways to go about merging two stories into one.

Interviews from well-loved authors, insightful analyses of two time-slip novels, and valuable worksheets make this thorough book an absolute must for any writer considering (or actively) writing split time novels."

—Heidi Chiavaroli, award-winning author of *The Tea Chest* and *Freedom's Ring*

"This book is a gold mine of information for those looking to write split time fiction. I honestly wish I'd had access to this knowledge when I started. Melanie and Morgan do a wonderful job of breaking down the basics and delving into the specifics for those who want to go deeper. Highly recommend!"

—Lindsay Harrel, best-selling author of *The Secrets of Paper and Ink*

"*A Split in Time* has earned a prominent place on my bookshelf. I have read several of the books mentioned and love the way they were analyzed. Each was broken down into easy-to-understand steps so the basic method could be mimicked if you prefer that particular style.

My first novel is a contemporary split time separated only by a few years. I wish I'd had *A Split in Time* before I began writing it. This book makes me want to write another split time novel.

I cannot wait to try the checklist, worksheets, and exercises that the authors have included at the end of the book. Thank you, Morgan and Melanie. You are an inspiration!"

—Carole Lehr Johnson, debut author of *Permelia Cottage*

"Dobson and Smith's brief manual is a compelling, engaging gem that reads as smoothly as the authors' novels. Well-organized, with detailed, helpful information about each identified component of split time fiction. The authors present examples in a way that clearly illustrates the teaching points, which isn't always easy to accomplish.

I will return to this manual again and again to underline and highlight as I draft my first split time novel. Nearly one-quarter of the book contains hands-on exercises to help readers become authors of their own split time stories.

If you enjoy reading time-slip fiction and are ready to try your hand at writing your own, run, don't walk, to buy this manual. Concise and step-by-step helpful from a team of award-winning split time authors." —Tracie Heskett, multi-published author

Introduction

WHY DO WE WRITE SPLIT TIME FICTION?

Morgan Tarpley Smith

The first time I read split time fiction was in early 2012 when my writing partner introduced me to an incredible novel that merged contemporary and historical storylines set by a castle along the Scottish coast. I savored **The Winter Sea** and was so grabbed by Susanna Kearsley's beautiful writing and the weaving of her two storylines that the majority of books I've read since then have been in this style.

What initially drew me to this type of novel was the weaving of present and past together. I have always loved history and how it connects to my present. It's the feeling of not losing our connection to our own ancestral past or that of our country and world in general.

Through fiction we not only preserve this past but also make history come alive for our readers, opening their minds and hearts to the important truths that it has to offer us, truths that remain relevant in the present.

It's always interesting for me to pick up a new novel and see how the author carries out this multi-story weaving.

Do they use third person point of view for all storylines? Or is one of their storylines in first person? Is it structured chapter by chapter or with multiple chapters in one storyline at a time?

Penning time-slip fiction is not for the faint of heart. It is complex, essentially writing two novels within 90,000 to 100,000 words. We have plenty of tips and advice to offer along your journey, but don't take it from just Melanie and me. Further in this book, you'll hear directly from some of the most popular split time authors in publishing. Each of them has a fascinating take on this burgeoning genre, and it's our hope you will glean valuable knowledge to decide if this genre is right for you.

Then, if the answer is yes, how to proceed. In essence, this is the book I wish I would have had years ago to help me navigate this challenging yet beautiful writing style.

Melanie Dobson

More than twenty years ago, I attempted to write my first novel by stitching together the threads from two plots—a past story about a woman who disappeared in Colorado's mining country and a contemporary one about her great-granddaughter trying to discover where she went.

I sent my manuscript to a dozen or so publishers and received back the same number of rejections. The general consensus—I needed to rip out the seams and rewrite, but I wasn't sure how to sew the dual timelines back together again.

So I tucked away my idea along with a stack of drafts and began writing a contemporary novel about a failed adoption that happened decades earlier. After seven years of trying to publish fiction, my first novel came out in 2005, and I followed that book with several historical and contemporary novels that featured characters searching for answers from the past.

Then something magical happened.

In 2008, **Sarah's Key** debuted in the United States. This novel by Tatiana de Rosnay wove together equally compelling past and present plotlines. Instead of having a character travel through time, the truth about a past character ultimately transformed the contemporary protagonist's life.

It was exactly what I wanted to write!

So I hunkered back down, studied the seams and structure of Tatiana's brilliant book, and began writing another novel set in both the past and present—this one about a French woman during World War II who hid members of the resistance in tunnels under her family's chateau. After I'd dreamed for years about publishing a past/present story, I was deeply honored when **Chateau of Secrets** won the Carol Award for Historical Fiction in 2015. Since then, I've written five time-slip novels.

In the past decade, dozens of novelists have begun weaving together past and present timelines, and according to *Publisher's Weekly*, this trend is continuing to grow.

In a recent article, Karen Watson of Tyndale House said, "There seems to be an ongoing interest in storytelling that bridges or twists traditional concepts of time and history. Rather than just straight linear historical fiction, we see a lot of novels that bridge two periods of time—what we call time-slip stories."

Thank you for joining us on this journey. We hope the following pages will inspire and encourage you with the information and resources needed to either write the time-slip story that's captured your heart or edit the one that you've already poured out on paper.

Our hope is that, as a result of all our work, this emerging genre will keep growing! Together we can continue creating and publishing split time novels for decades to come.

Chapter One

WHAT IS SPLIT TIME FICTION?

In every time-slip novel, we have to choose a starting point. A moment to launch our readers and characters on an unforgettable journey that spans across time.

But how do we launch a book about writing split time fiction? We are both passionate about this genre and have so many things we want to discuss—the suggested elements of a time-slip novel, how to weave together multiple story-lines, the things to avoid. We also want to share the many tricks we've learned from our years of reading, studying, and writing this genre.

It's the terminology, though, that is often the most confusing for all of us, so we've opted to start by clarifying several things.

Split time novels, by definition, **consist of two or more storylines.** In this book we are going to navigate together the challenge of writing a novel with two or more storylines and provide tools, resources, and insight from fellow authors to help you master this craft.

One thing that we aren't going to navigate is what to

call this melding together of two or more time periods into one cohesive story since publishers, authors, and readers call the multiple timeline format by multiple names. *Split time. Twin strand. Time jump. Time split. Hybrid. Time slip. Dual timeframe* or *parallel timeline* for those books with two story-lines. *Multi-timeline* for those that have more than two.

Nor are we going to attempt to resolve the debate about which of these compound adjectives to hyphenate. Our expertise is on the creative side of writing, so we've decided to punctuate these terms based on how other publishers and authors use them, a structure that continues to evolve.

While there is currently no set term or punctuation for this rapidly growing genre, we prefer **split time** or **time-slip fiction**—this idea of stitching together two or more stories as readers *(not the characters)* slip through time. Other writers may use other terms, and this diversity represents the many possibilities for this genre. And we love to dream about the possibilities!

It doesn't really matter to us what we call it.

> ***The important thing is that readers continue
> to be swept away by stories
> that transport them seamlessly across time.***

One more clarification before we dive in…

A split time novel typically has a contemporary and a historical timeline. The difference between a "contemporary" plotline and a "historical" plotline can be a bit murky if part of your novel is set in, say, 1976. Some of us shudder to think of 1976 as the past, while others will think the 1970s are ancient history.

In this book, we will use the terms "contemporary" and

"historical" to represent a past and present plotline. The story most current and then one further in the past even if the past is just a decade ago. This way we can capture the broad scope of our genre in novels like Mesu Andrews' time-slip ***Of Fire and Lions*** where the contemporary plot is set in 539 B.C. Or in Erin Bartel's ***The Words Between Us*** as present-day character Robin reflects on a parallel storyline that follows her twenty years earlier.

The following pages will provide tips on how to write this genre, essential elements for your story, examples to review, interviews with other split time writers, and practical resources to help structure your ideas. Whether you are a seasoned writer ready for a new journey or a first-time novelist wanting to learn the split timeline format, we hope this book will provide the necessary skills to weave two or more compelling stories into one time-slip novel.

Chapter Two

IS THIS GENRE RIGHT FOR YOU?

WRITING split time fiction is hard. ***Really*** hard. But weaving together past and present plots has become one of the greatest joys of my (Melanie's) life. In fact, after writing seven time-slip novels, it's become difficult for me to write straight historical fiction. I want to know what happens long after my past plotline is finished.

I want to know the end of the story!

Morgan and I have put together a list of questions below to help you determine if this genre is right for you because launching into dual timeline is about more than just technique. Writing time-slip fiction requires an incredible amount of curiosity. The kind that almost everyone else, except a fellow writer, will think strange.

For example, do you walk into an old house and wish desperately the walls could whisper their secrets? Do you look at an antique steamer trunk and wonder at its voyage?

Do you actually like visiting cemeteries to read the epitaphs of those who've gone before us?

Do you ever resolve a past mystery by making up your own story?

Like many of you, I often wonder about the story behind furnishings left in an abandoned house or an unusual inscription on a gravestone. The wondering haunts me until I uncover the facts or sort it out through fiction.

A reader friend recently shared her grandmother Susan's story with me. Susan never held any public position or taught a class or generated an audience on social media. But she loved well and shared her life with a multitude of people. Now a host of women named Suze, Susie, and Susan are continuing her legacy in both private and public positions, loving people like she did. The story —*the impact*—of her life will continue on for generations.

That's what we as time-slip novelists want to know. How someone's story impacted others, for good or bad. How the threads of his or her life wove together either a terrible web or a beautiful tapestry for the next generations. How they changed their world.

If you're still not certain this genre is right for you, take a few moments to think through your answers to the following questions:

- Do you enjoy reading novels with both past and present plots?
- Do you like writing both historical and contemporary fiction?

- Do you long to understand the results of a decision or situation that happened years ago?
- Does the thought of discovering an unforgettable connection between the past and present day excite you?
- Do you like to research?
- Are you ready for a challenge?
- Can you embrace the old proverb: *If at first you don't succeed, try, try again?*

For beginning writers...

If you haven't written a full-length novel yet, we'd recommend you complete a straight contemporary or historical novel before diving into the split time genre, but if you are ready to begin this journey, we are thrilled to help equip you with the techniques you need to accomplish this challenge.

For seasoned writers...

Perhaps you have written several or even published many contemporary and/or historical novels, and you are intrigued by split time. Perhaps you're even penning your first novel within this style. It will be an exciting new challenge for you to write two novels within one.

We asked several successful authors why they enjoy writing time-split fiction. Leslie Gould says she writes it to explore the past and its impact on her family as well as other families and time periods. Cathy Gohlke, a multi-published historical novelist, decided to write a split time novel to wrestle with questions close to her heart.

"We can repent and receive forgiveness for our sins," Cathy says, "but how do we address the sins of our parents or grandparents—sin and shame that have shaped or still affect our lives and/or the lives of others?

"Because this involved both what happened in the past and how we deal with the present, I needed to tell both sides of the story, really get into the heads of those living with the crimes of the past and those dealing with the fallout in more recent times. Writing a dual timeline was the only way I knew to fully explore all sides of the characters and the relevant questions."

Regardless, whether you have written little or much within fiction, if the past—or the potential of a past story—haunts you (in the best sense of the word), if you are ready and willing to immerse yourself into multiple plots, if you are excited about reading time-slip fiction and rewriting as much as you write, then this just might be the genre for you.

Together, we are going to uncover how to create a time-slip story that you will enjoy (on most days) writing. And a story that your readers will love!

Chapter Three

KEYS TO WRITE TIME-SLIP FICTION

WEAVING TOGETHER two stories into one novel is a rewarding challenge, but it can also feel overwhelming at times. While each time-slip story is unique, the key components remain the same.

***Below are thirteen elements to help direct
the structure of your manuscript.***

- Multiple Time Periods
- Contemporary Characters Solving Past Mysteries
- A Past and Present Protagonist
- Different Points of View
- Conflict and Character Arc in Both Past and Present Plots
- Bridge to the Past
- Compelling Reason to Solve Mystery NOW
- Backstory Is Front Story
- TELL in Present Story, SHOW in Past Story

- Foreshadow Past Plot through Present
- Passing the Baton
- Mirror Theme/Premise in Past and Present
- Stories Collide Near the End

Multiple Time Periods

A split time novel must have multiple storylines in more than one time period. Some even feature three or four time periods, but if this is your first novel, two should be enough.

Time-slip novels can begin with either a past or present chapter, and some begin with a prologue. Like with any well-written historical novel, the past story should start with immediacy—something urgent is about to happen—and then slip into the present timeline as the protagonist begins a journey to discover what happened long ago.

If the split time novel begins in the present day, the story typically will jump to the past after the first two or three chapters such as with Kristy Cambron's ***The Butterfly and the Violin***, Lisa Wingate's ***The Story Keeper***, Susanna Kearsley's ***A Desperate Fortune***, and Heidi Chiavaroli's ***The Tea Chest***.

Time-slip novels that start with the past story should follow the same format and move to the present after the first few chapters such as with Jaime Jo Wright's ***The House on Foster Hill***, Kate Morton's ***The Forgotten Garden***, Kristy Cambron's ***The Painted Castle***, and Rachel Hauck's ***The Love Letter***.

When it comes to the actual writing of the storylines, each author has their own writing process, sometimes even changing their method for different novels. Some novelists write one thread, then they combine it with the past or present story. Melanie writes both storylines together in her time-slip manuscripts. Morgan writes the first few chapters of the present story and then the entire past storyline before weaving in the remaining present chapters. Other authors compile a jumble of scenes and intertwine them later.

Heidi Chiavaroli always starts her books with the contemporary storyline.

> "I don't think there's a right or a wrong way, but I tend to ground myself by starting with the present-day," she says. "It gives me perspective on where my contemporary characters are in their journey, where they will end up, and how they will change with the help of my historical characters. More often than not, it will also give me a lens in which to better view my historical story."

In contrast, Leslie Gould writes each of her split time novels differently, sometimes writing one whole storyline and intertwining the other or writing the opening contemporary chapters and then writing the entire historical storyline or intertwining the storylines as she goes. She chooses the approach that inspires her to write the fastest, keeping the writing process fresh for her.

Most of Susan Meissner's dual storylines have been written simultaneously since she learns about the main characters by actually writing their story. She is almost always inspired, she says, by a historical context of some kind, but she doesn't always start writing the historical storyline first in her novels.

"I try to make all my decisions for the story's good, not my own. My preferences always have to be second to the story's needs. I don't think of myself as a slave to the story, though. I am still the master of the narrative; I just choose to make decisions on what is best for the story, not what is easiest or best or preferred by me."

How you write and structure the back and forth is up to you, but the following are three common formats to smoothly transition between time periods:

- Staccato story
- Sandwich story
- Sectional story

The **staccato format** is how Melanie typically writes time-slip fiction. Chapters in this structure tend to be shorter than the other styles as the plot shifts quickly between past and present threads. The timelines may seem disjointed at first, but as the story progresses, the connection between past and present becomes clear.

In ***The Lost Castle***, Kristy Cambron intertwines three storylines—a present-day one and two historical—and switches equally between each one. She also uses this same format for the other two books in the series—***Castle on the Rise*** and ***The Painted Castle***. Lisa Wingate writes a staccato-type story in her best-selling novel, ***Before We Were Yours***, as she weaves together the stories of a girl trapped in a web of deceit during the 1930s and a modern-day heroine who begins to uncover a tragedy from long ago.

The **sandwich format** (what some call a *frame*

structure) is a time-slip story where the beginning and end are usually contemporary while the middle pages contain the past story. ***The Nightingale*** by Kristin Hannah is an excellent example of a sandwich story. In this novel about two sisters, readers have a contemporary glimpse of a woman about to receive an award for her work during World War II. We don't know which sister survived the war until the end of the book.

The **sectional format** contains a long section of one storyline and then switches to a long section from the other story, weaving them together like the staccato format except readers stay grounded in the past and then present for longer periods of time. Leslie Gould and Mindy Starns Clark's **Cousins of the Dove** series and ***A Fall of Marigolds*** by Susan Meissner use this sectional structure, so readers can settle in for multiple chapters before changing time periods.

In another example of a sectional story, ***The Tea Chest*** by Heidi Chiavaroli follows this pattern of present and past chapters:

- Prologue & Chapter 1 (present)
- Chapters 2-6 (past)
- Chapters 7-9 (present)
- Chapters 10-17 (past)
- Chapters 18-21 (present)
- Chapters 22-24 (past)
- Chapters 25-31 (present)
- Chapters 32-39 (past)
- Chapters 40-43 (present)

Heidi's chapter lengths vary throughout the novel from

around 1,000 words to 3,500 words as each new piece of information propels the story forward.

Any of these formats work well for a time-slip story. Do you have a preference for one of the above three? If not, you can create an entirely new format for your novel.

Contemporary Characters Solving Past Mysteries

The beauty of the split time genre is that our readers learn what happened long ago through a compelling story instead of dialogue. As the novel progresses, our contemporary protagonist should become highly motivated to discover something that happened in the past.

In **_Sarah's Key_**, for example, the past protagonist (Sarah) is searching for her brother after French police deported her family during World War II. This mystery incites the contemporary heroine—a woman named Julia—to find out more until Julia becomes determined to uncover what happened. As readers begin to discover the truth about Sarah's brother in the contemporary story, they are also watching the story unfold in the historical thread.

There are varying types of mystery found within split time novels. Some examples are:

Echoes Among the Stones
by Jaime Jo Wright—a murder

The Forgotten Seamstress
by Liz Trenow—a lost child

The Tea Chest
by Heidi Chiavaroli—a tea chest

The Lost Castle
by Kristy Cambron—a forgotten castle

Memories of Glass
by Melanie Dobson—a family legacy

The Wedding Dress
by Rachel Hauck—a wedding dress

Bellewether
by Susanna Kearsley—an old house

Not all time-slip novels have a mystery component, but an unsolved mystery from the past will keep readers engaged in both the historical and contemporary stories as well as the connection between them.

A Past and Present Protagonist

Instead of one hero or heroine, the split time genre typically has a contemporary and a historical protagonist. These protagonists should want something throughout the novel, and they will do almost anything to achieve their goals. In order for the story to flow smoothly, readers should care deeply about the conflict and success of both protagonists .

"Each point of view character," Rachel Hauck says, "must have all the elements of a great protagonist: a problem, obstacles, wants, goals, epiphany, black moment, overcoming, and happy ending. You can't shortchange any of the characters."

In ***The House on Foster Hill***, the contemporary heroine's husband supposedly died in a tragic accident, and her suspicions that he was murdered fall on deaf ears. In the past storyline, the heroine faces death too, but it is that of a stranger—a young woman found murdered at the house on Foster Hill, the same house that the contemporary heroine purchases sight unseen. Both past and present heroines face danger when the house's dark history surfaces, but they won't let anything stop them from discovering the truth.

One exception to this rule is found in ***The Last Year of the War*** by Susan Meissner. While the story is split between multiple time periods, it follows the same heroine through the years instead of a past and present-day character.

Different Points of View

Novels are written through the perspective of one or more characters in the first-person or third-person point of view. Often a story will be told from the perspective of various characters through the use of third person, but some novelists opt to tell a character's first-person perspective The key is to show each main character's story in a way that will capture readers.

The contemporary section in ***Memories of Glass*** begins with Ava Kingston's first-person point of view: *Memories are curious things. Some I want to remember, and others . . . well, I simply don't. Most of my memories—at least the ones from childhood—are curdled into lumps anyway. No amount of stirring will separate them.*

This first-person perspective, written in present tense,

launches readers into Ava's story as she begins to navigate her family's tragic journey during and after World War II. There are multiple points of view in the historical timeline, but each chapter is written from one character's perspective in the third person, past tense.

In time-slip fiction, there are a variety of POV combinations. All storylines might be written in third person or perhaps all in first person. Some novels, like ***Memories of Glass***, contain a mix of first person and third. Rarer are novels with both storylines in first person, but Heidi Chiavaroli does this in ***The Tea Chest***.

One of the major pitfalls in using first person in multiple storylines can be that the character's voices, whether in dialogue or thought, sound too similar. According to Cathy Gohlke, who wrote dual first person storylines in ***Secrets She Kept***, "create unique inner voices as well as appropriate dialect in dialogue for your characters, making certain those voices reflect the two different time periods." Both Heidi and Cathy did an excellent job of differentiating the first-person point of views for each of their main protagonists.

Often we have to write the first chapters of our novel from different perspectives before we land on which character and point of view will be most effective to tell the story. If the point of view for your story doesn't seem to be working, try rewriting a scene or chapter in the opposite point of view. Read both versions aloud to listen to your character's voice. By experimenting, we can see which perspective best fits the storyline.

Below are some examples of how point of view is used in the following split time novels. The "contemporary" timeline, as we mentioned above, refers to the most current plot and "historical" refers to the one further in the past.

***

My Brother's Crown by Leslie Gould and Mindy Clark
Contemporary storyline is first person and the past is third.

Echoes Among the Stones by Jaime Jo Wright
Contemporary and past storylines are third person.

A Fall of Marigolds by Susan Meissner
Contemporary and past storylines are first person.

The Lost Castle by Kristy Cambron
Contemporary and two past timelines are third person.

Freedom's Ring by Heidi Chiavaroli
Contemporary and past storylines are first person.

The Winter Sea by Susanna Kearsley
Contemporary storyline is first person, the past is third.

The Wedding Dress by Rachel Hauck
Contemporary and historical timelines are third person.

Whose Waves These Are by Amanda Dykes
Both storylines are in third person, present tense.

The Forgotten Garden by Kate Morton
Contemporary and past storylines are in third person.

Conflict and Character Arc in Both Past & Present Plots

This is where the time-slip genre gets even more challenging to write, but it's a fun challenge. The main characters in both the past and present should have goals and what happens over the course of their stories, what they discover along the way, should change them and their goals profoundly.

The contemporary protagonist's main external goal is often to find out what happened in the past, but what she discovers should change her internally as well. Whatever happened in the past will forever alter her mindset and present circumstances.

One of the most important keys to weaving together great time-slip fiction is this—the past discovery should rock our hero or heroine off their axis and send him or her spinning in an entirely new direction. It will change their present and probably their future.

Lisa Wingate's dual timeline novel ***Before We Were Yours*** quickly became a *New York Times* bestseller with more than two million copies sold in its first three years. In this story, the contemporary heroine is an attorney and daughter of an affluent senator. A woman in a nursing home steals Avery's bracelet, and when she meets this woman, Avery is launched on a new journey to unearth her story. By the end of the book, Avery is a different person as a result of what she discovers—the tragic events at the Tennessee Children's Home Society eighty years earlier and the stories of children who survived. Stories that change her and her family.

In ***A Fall of Marigolds***, both protagonists—Taryn (present) and Clara (past)—are reeling from similar pasts and carry trauma from losing a loved one, living in the in-between world of life and death, unable to move on and release the past. Throughout the novel, we discover bits and pieces about what happened to them and the depth of their shared desire/goal—to return to the present after their traumatic experiences and losses. It is that desire that drives the storylines for each character and therefore intertwines their journeys, culminating in Taryn's change after learning Clara's story.

Bridge to Past

Usually a token or symbol ties together the past and present in split time fiction. This object is a bridge, in a sense, so the contemporary character has something tangible to remind her of what happened long ago.

Sometimes a diary or old letters contain the past story, but often an heirloom or another tangible piece links the past and present, an item that would be treasured in both time periods for either its sentimental or monetary value.

"With split time, there's usually an object or event which anchors the story," Rachel Hauck says. "What is that 'thing' that existed in the past yet has impact in the present?"

Rachel Hauck has used items like a wedding dress and a desk as bridges to the past. Items that readers might empathize with because of cherished possessions within their own family.

Lisa Wingate also employs a physical connection between her characters through an object, a place, or a written record like letters in a prayer box.

"In my novel, **_The Story Keeper_**, the connection between a modern-day editor and a Melungeon girl in turn-of-the-century Appalachia is an old partial manuscript that lands unexpectedly on an editor's desk. Her search for the rest of the manuscript takes her on a journey back to the Blue Ridge."

In Heidi Chiavaroli's novel **_Freedom's Ring_**, an old ring connects the contemporary characters with characters from the colonial era. In **_The Curse of Misty Wayfair_** by Jaime Jo Wright, an old photograph bridges the contemporary character to the past. In **_The Butterfly and the Violin_**, a hidden painting brings together a Manhattan art dealer and the decades-old story of an Austrian violinist.

All very different split time concepts, but each novel has a bridge that is essential to connecting the past and present.

Compelling Reason to Solve Mystery NOW

Sometimes the contemporary characters stumble onto the past mystery and sometimes an event prompts them to search for information. No matter how the story launches, this mystery thread quickly becomes a pressing matter.

What has happened in the present to make resolving a mystery urgent for your contemporary characters?

The information might be needed to save someone's life or livelihood. Maybe the contemporary protagonist has just discovered a story about an ancestor or receives an inheritance or is gifted an object that sends her on an unexpected journey to learn more. And she will not stop until she knows the truth!

Just like in a contemporary or historical novel, an inciting incident is the catalyst to hook our readers, followed by a point of no return where the characters are forced to continue their journey.

If you're not familiar with terms like *inciting incident* or *point of no return*, here are a few recommended books about these essential writing elements:

- ***Plot & Structure*** by James Scott Bell
- ***Writing the Breakout Novel*** by Donald Maass
- ***Guide to Fiction Writing*** by Phyllis A. Whitney

A personal connection often emerges near the beginning of a time-slip novel that compels the contemporary character forward. In Melanie's novel ***Hidden Among the Stars***, the contemporary protagonist stumbles upon a list in an old children's book that launches her on a new journey. When she discovers a personal connection, it quickly becomes an urgent matter for her to locate the author of this list.

In ***Sarah's Key***, when the main character discovers that her husband's family moved into the same apartment where Sarah's family once lived, the apartment becomes the bridge to the past story.

In both these novels, the personal connection compels the contemporary heroines to seek out what happened in the 1940s.

Backstory Is Front Story

We don't want readers to get lost in long segments of backstory. While there is a lot of debate among novelists and editors about how much to use in a historical or contemporary novel, much of the backstory in time-slip fiction is our FRONT story (lots of cheering from those of us who love to write all those past details).

This is the beauty of writing time slip. We get to SHOW much of what happened in the historical plotline, and if we've built up intrigue and empathy for our characters, our readers will care deeply about what happened to them in the past.

Robin Lee Hatcher has written a series of split time novels called **Legacy of Faith**. The contemporary plot is different in each one, but the historical timeline and bridge of a family Bible follows the Henning family through the decades. In the first novel of this series, ***Who I Am With You***, Andrew Henning loses his banking job during the Great Depression. In this time-slip structure, we experience both heartache and hope alongside this family, their backstory becoming the reader's front story for the entire series.

TELL in Present Story, SHOW in Past Story

A familiar mantra for writers is: *"Show, don't tell your story,"* but this phrase can lead to all sorts of confusion because we can't possibly show everything that happens in a novel. This is particularly true about split time fiction.

We get to TELL part of our story through the contemporary plotline even as we show it happening in the past. Our contemporary characters can discuss and research the time period so our past story doesn't get bogged down in timeline details. Then our contemporary protagonist, in a sense, will pass the baton back to the historical protagonist to continue the story.

In ***The Butterfly and the Violin***, the contemporary protagonist, Sera, searches through numerous historical records for the Nazi concentration camps at Auschwitz to find any trace of the haunting woman she sees in a portrait. Sera is aware of the history of Auschwitz as well as how the war ends while the past protagonist, Adele, is in the midst of the conflict as her story unfolds. Adele has no idea who will be the victor in World War II.

Our contemporary characters have insight that those in the past won't have. As your contemporary characters learn more about specific events, readers will watch these events play out in the historical timeline.

Foreshadow Past Plot through Present

Foreshadowing is one of our favorite time-slip devices. We can plant clues about what's going to happen in the past story through the research or prior knowledge of our contemporary characters. While some of the details should be confusing for our characters in the beginning of the novel, our modern-day hero or heroine will gain insight about the past as the story progresses.

Once readers are engaged with our characters, once they know an important event is about to occur, this increases the conflict. The more the contemporary characters discover about the past, the more it ratchets up the tension because the reader knows the opposition the characters will face before they do.

This is the ebb and flow of split time. We can have an action scene from the past and then a reflective scene in the present where the contemporary character considers and perhaps researches an event from long ago. Often, because the modern characters spend time searching for answers, the past strand has more external conflict and action than the present story. With this structure, the present story can be a breather from the intensity, the place where more of the internal conflict is stirring.

The modern protagonist, for example, might need to heal from a past wound or try to mend a relationship through what she learns in the past. Both our contemporary and past protagonists should have internal conflict, but in most split time stories, the contemporary character will have a greater change based on what she discovers.

Anaya, the contemporary protagonist in ***Freedom's Ring,*** harbors both fear and guilt from her niece's injuries during the Boston Marathon bombing. In the past a woman named Liberty must also conquer fear and guilt as she grapples with political loyalties and a dangerous predicament amid the uproar surrounding the Boston Massacre (an event foreshadowed in Anaya's point of view as she walks through Boston, looking at painted reliefs about the Patriots who died there in 1770). These two women, separated by centuries, must learn to face their fears, and eventually they each learn that true strength is sometimes found in surrender. Anaya is forever changed by Liberty's story.

Our stories are like a dance with two partners who perfectly complement each other as they perform. No need to repeat steps or information as they glide across the floor. If the contemporary storyline isn't dependent on the past—and the tension in the historical plot isn't dependent on information from the present—the balance and connection is thrown off. Each plotline relies on the other to communicate the full breadth of story.

A quick warning here—we must be careful not to contradict a prior chapter or reveal something not yet ready to be revealed in the contemporary storyline. The bridge to the past, for example, might be shown in the historical section or it might be revealed first in the contemporary section to add mystery to its origins.

In ***Castle on the Rise*** by Kristy Cambron, the connection of a special piano is introduced in the past storyline *(spoiler alert)* and then discovered in the present hidden within the depths of an old Irish castle. The touching moment of the piano's reveal in the present day would have been lost on the reader if they didn't already know of its significance in the past.

Passing the Baton

One of the most effective ways to weave together a split time story is to pass the baton well between past and present stories. This is not a technique we should use for every chapter, but it's one that helps transition between multiple time periods without jarring the reader. If we are creative in this passing of our baton, readers may not even realize what we're doing. Instead they will appreciate the seamless transitions that keep them immersed in our stories.

The baton could be weather—a storm might threaten our characters at the end of a contemporary chapter and then we pan straight over to a storm in the historical portion. The baton could be similar dialogue or décor or a situation that transcends time. Anything to transport readers smoothly between the storylines.

Kate Mosse used this technique perfectly near the end of her book ***The Labyrinth*** *(another spoiler alert here)*. This novel is split between two summers—one that starts in 1209 and one in 2005. Alice Tanner, the contemporary heroine, stumbles onto a medieval mystery when she volunteers for an archeological dig in France. The story flashes back to the Crusades and a young woman who holds the secret to locating the Holy Grail.

In **Chapter 80**, the contemporary characters sprint into a cave:

> *Before Alice had realized what was happening, someone had grabbed her from behind. She screamed and kicked out, but there were two of them.*
>
> *It happened like this before. Then someone called her name. Not Audric.*
>
> *A wave of nausea swept over her and she started to fall. "Catch her, you idiots," Marie-Cécile shouted.*

The chapter ends at the edge of a cliff (literally and figuratively), and Mosse passes the baton smoothly to the historical characters at the beginning of **Chapter 81**:

> *Guilhem couldn't catch Alaïs. She was already too far ahead.*
>
> *He staggered down the tunnel in the dark. Pain pierced his side where his ribs were cracked…*

This is a brilliant transition between time periods. Both the past and present heroines are being chased, their lives threatened. And we must keep reading to find out whether the past or present character will be caught.

Another example—in ***Hidden Among the Stars***, the contemporary heroine (Callie) finishes a scene by picking up her cat and watching a Memorial Day parade outside her window. The chapter ends and the next chapter begins from the perspective of Max, the historical hero.

Gray cobblestones pressed into Max Dornbach's knees as he knelt in an alley near Heldenplatz and scratched Frederica, the stray tabby cat he'd befriended, behind her ears. A peaceful ruler, her name meant. And right now, they desperately needed der Frieden in Austria.

Max is off to a parade as well except it is a mandatory one to welcome Adolf Hitler into Austria. In this transition, the cat and the parade are used as batons to pass readers back into a historical scene. Different characters and time period but shared experiences for these characters.

Another effective way to pass the baton between past and present sections is to add the date, setting, and/or character names to the beginning of each chapter. And, potentially, visual cues through a unique design in the chapter headings to differentiate between contemporary and historical chapters. Some readers might say this is distracting, but many appreciate subtle cues like this so they can stay immersed in the story.

Mirror Theme/Premise in Past & Present

The terms "theme" and "premise" are often used interchangeably among writers and teachers. A story theme is a universal concept or message like love, faith, or finding identity. A reflection (usually) of our personal beliefs and worldview.

When someone asks what our book is about, often we'll tell them about this underlying meaning. *It's a story*—we might say—*about two high school sweethearts reunited after twenty years.* Reconciliation and love are the themes here.

Our characters in both the past and present stories should be wrestling with the same themes as we tie the plotlines together. They might have to decide if they want to embrace grief as in ***A Fall of Marigolds***, redemption in ***Castle on the Rise***, or true freedom like Emma and Hayley in ***The Tea Chest***.

"What is the thing that weaves the two stories together?" Cathy Gohlke asks. "This common thread will create a roadmap—a pathway along which your chosen theme will reveal itself through our characters' experiences and their reactions to those experiences."

After we determine the themes, we can dive even deeper into the heart of our stories by utilizing a **moral premise** from the resource ***The Moral Premise: Harnessing Virtue & Vice for Box Office Success*** by Stanley Williams.

The basic structure for a moral premise is:

(NEGATIVE CHOICE) ____________________

*leads to (VICE)*__________________________,

*but (POSITIVE CHOICE)*__________________

*leads to (VIRTUE)*_____________________.

When our characters make a negative choice, they will have a negative consequence based on our selected vice. The positive choices will result in a predetermined virtue.

The device of a moral premise is particularly important for time-slip fiction because the protagonists in both the past and present plots **AND** the antagonist(s) should wrestle with one virtue and one opposing vice that transcends time.

In the end, all our main characters should be given a choice between the selected vice and virtue. The protagonist will ultimately choose the VIRTUE and our antagonist will ultimately choose the VICE.

Based on this structure, the moral premise for Melanie's novel ***Catching the Wind*** is:

Unforgiveness leads to a lifetime of regret (vice), but forgiveness leads to the restoration of relationships (virtue).

Quenby, the protagonist in the contemporary plot, has a relationship with her mother that is seemingly beyond repair. Dietmar, the historical protagonist, lost his dear friend Brigitte in England before World War II and has spent much of his life searching for her.

Every main character in ***Catching the Wind*** has a choice to make. They can either proactively restore their broken relationships or refuse to forgive.

Not all of the characters who choose to forgive in ***Catching the Wind*** are reunited, but their relationships are restored in other ways. The antagonists in both the past and present storylines have an opportunity for restoration, but they choose the vice (*unforgiveness*) instead of the virtue. As a result, they face regret and brokenness for a lifetime.

> ***If this information about moral premises is literary Greek to you—and you don't own a copy of Stanley Williams' book—order* The Moral Premise *right now and then head back our way.***

No one else will see our moral premise, but it should be the guiding light of our stories, the focus of our message. When we don't know what dilemma a character should face, we can turn to our moral premise to decide what's next in both the past and present.

If we determine, for example, that selfishness leads to defeat and sacrificial love leads to success, both our past and present protagonists will have to choose between selfishness and sacrificial love. In the end, if good triumphs over evil, the hero or heroine will have to choose sacrificial love.

By successfully utilizing a premise, we will have the perfect seam between past and present. Our readers probably won't realize that our characters are choosing between the same virtue and vice, but the impact of this should be like dynamite to the heart (okay, maybe not the best analogy, but tears should follow the struggle and success of your characters).

And when we don't know what to write next, when we inevitably get stuck in the middle, we can return to our moral premise. Armed with this, we can decide what our characters are facing next and specifically what will happen if our characters make the right choice and what will happen if they make the wrong one.

Stories Collide Near the End

The stories of the contemporary and past protagonists will intersect at some point in a split time novel, often with a huge collision when the present-day character discovers a secret or something that has affected him or her personally. The fireworks that ensue and then reconciliation should be the main focus of our last pages.

Maybe someone is NOT who the contemporary character thought he or she was. Or the past events were not as they originally seemed. In stories where the time periods are just decades apart, often someone from the past can emerge into the contemporary story to surprise both the reader and contemporary protagonist.

In **_The Secret Keeper_**, Kate Morton weaves the stories of her main characters together in a brilliant twist as the mysteries of the past reveal themselves and resolve the many questions raised along the way. The clues are planted in both the contemporary and historical timelines, but readers don't know how they fit together until the end.

Almost every thread should be stitched up in the last third of our books (we say "almost" because some writers like to leave one or two threads dangling for readers to stitch together themselves). All the major plot points should be resolved, and in those last pages, both protagonists will have to wrestle through the moral premise one last time and make a final choice between the vice and virtue.

This is the point of the novel where readers realize why this story had to be told from two time periods and at least two different perspectives. One plotline would not have given them the same emotional journey. Our story needed a present and past timeline for the fireworks, the tears, the "aha!" moment in our conclusion.

In the end, the past story can be revealed to the present protagonist in different ways. The protagonist could learn the entire truth or just enough to be greatly affected by it.

Some examples of these final connections between present and past include:

The Butterfly and the Violin by Kristy Cambron
A spoken story

The Forgotten Garden by Kate Morton
An unearthed discovery

The Tea Chest by Heidi Chiavaroli
Historical tidbits in research
as well as letters and diary entries

A Fall of Marigolds by Susan Meissner
An old letter

The Forgotten Seamstress by Liz Trenow
Taped recordings and a letter

Memories of Glass by Melanie Dobson
Historical research, a conversation, and a surprise event

WITH EVERY RULE ARE EXCEPTIONS, of course, and we realize that not every published time-slip novel includes all thirteen components. The successful stories, however, have most (and often all) of these pieces.

How exactly do these elements play out in a full-length novel?

In the next section, we will analyze two time-slip novels in light of these components, and at the end of the book are several worksheets so you can analyze your manuscript and other split time stories.

**For a list of recent split time books
to review, visit:**

splittimefiction.com
morgantarpleysmith.com
Goodreads group and bookshelf,
Split Time Fiction That Travels

Chapter Four

SPLIT TIME NOVEL ANALYSIS

WHOSE WAVES THESE ARE
BY AMANDA DYKES

BELOW IS a breakdown of the key split time elements in Amanda Dykes' literary debut **Whose Waves These Are**. We've tried not to include any major spoilers within this section because reading this beautifully written novel is an experience we don't want you to miss.

Before we start analyzing, here is a little more about this story.

> In the wake of WWII, a grieving fisherman submits a poem to a local newspaper: a rallying cry for hope, purpose . . . and rocks. *Send me a rock for the person you lost, and I will build something life-giving.* When the poem spreads farther than he ever intended, Robert Bliss's humble words change the tide of a nation.

Boxes of rocks inundate the tiny, coastal Maine town, and he sets his calloused hands to work, but the building halts when tragedy strikes.

Decades later, Annie Bliss is summoned back to Ansel-by-the-Sea when she learns her Great-Uncle Robert, the man who became her refuge during the hardest summer of her youth, is now the one in need of help. What she didn't anticipate was finding a wall of heavy boxes hiding in his home. Long-ago memories of stone ruins on a nearby island trigger her curiosity, igniting a fire in her anthropologist soul to uncover answers.

She joins forces with the handsome and mysterious harbor postman, and all her hopes of mending the decades-old chasm in her family seem to point back to the ruins. But with Robert failing fast, her search for answers battles against time, a foe as relentless as the ever-crashing waves upon the sea.

A huge thank you to Amanda for allowing us to break down her story like this:

Multiple Time Periods

World War II and the contemporary plot (set in 2001) are the two major time periods in *Whose Waves These Are*. While the story begins in World War II, it continues through the decades until the past collides with the present.

Contemporary Characters Solving Past Mysteries

The contemporary heroine Annie Bliss is intent on helping her father and her great-uncle reconcile their relationship. In order to do this, she must find out what happened between the men decades ago.

Amanda uses the ***sectional format*** in this novel with a greater focus on the contemporary story as Annie is trying to reconcile what happened in the past. While much of the story is focused on Annie's personal healing, Amanda slowly develops the past mystery by giving readers a little information at a time about what happened between the uncle and nephew (Annie's dad).

A Past and Present Protagonist

Annie is the present protagonist, and Robert, her great-uncle, is the past. Robert is still alive in the contemporary scenes, but he is in a coma at the beginning of the book—the inciting incident that brings Annie back to Ansel-by-the-Sea. The reader cares deeply about what happens to both protagonists.

Different Points of View

The contemporary sections are written in third person from Annie's perspective, and the historical plot is third person from Robert's point of view. One unique element in this story is that both the present and past threads are written in the immediate present tense.

Conflict and Character Arc in Both Past & Present Plots

The past and present stories are filled with compelling conflict—romance, war, loss, and enduring love. Both protagonists also have a character arc to complete.

In the contemporary plot, Annie needs to forgive herself for something that happened in her work as an anthropologist. She also needs to learn how to relate directly to people, not just study them. As readers, we aren't certain if Robert is going to survive to complete his character arc, but he needs to forgive himself for what happened in the past and learn how to relate to his loved ones in the present day.

As in any split-time novel where the past and contemporary storylines merge, Robert and Annie need each other to complete their individual journeys.

Bridge to the Past

In this novel, the bridge between the present and past is a crumbling lighthouse made of stones shipped by people from around the world who lost someone during the war. In the past storyline, Robert was never able to complete the lighthouse, but as the story unfolds, Annie is determined to know why he stopped building the lighthouse and how they can restore it.

Compelling Reason to Solve Mystery NOW

Because we like Robert and want him to reconcile with his nephew, we are cheering for Annie to solve the mystery of this broken relationship as soon as possible. Annie is compelled to resolve this mystery NOW, because she wants restoration before Robert passes away.

Backstory Is Front Story

This novel has a compelling backstory of love and loss and then love again. If the love story portions had been written as backstory in a contemporary novel, it wouldn't have been nearly as captivating in chunks of "telling" paragraphs and backflash scenes. Instead we read the past action as it unfolds in a story format and keep turning these pages to find out happens to Robert in both the past and present.

TELL in Present Story, SHOW in Past Story

Some of the details in the present story are easily told instead of shown. In one example, Amanda *shows* us what happened in the past when Robert loses the love of his life. Then she *tells* us in the present story about the resolution when Robert begins to love again. We are thrilled to know that Robert finds love one more time even though we don't yet know how. The story then slips back into the past, and Amanda *shows* us how Robert met the woman he'd eventually marry.

Foreshadow Past Plot through Present

In the contemporary plot, we learn that Robert is estranged from most of his family, but he is also a very likable guy. We can't imagine why his family doesn't want to be with him. We know early on that there is a problem through Amanda's present-day foreshadowing, and then we begin to see the unfolding of what happened in the past. It's believable that the past situation wounded the relationships in this family, and the beauty of split time fiction is that not only do we get to see what happened long ago, we step into the story decades later to cheer for Robert's success as these old wounds begin to heal.

Passing the Baton

Because this story has about four chapters in each past or present section, there isn't as much opportunity (like in a staccato format) to pass the baton, but Amanda still transitions smoothly between these past and present sections.

At the end of Chapter 9, two contemporary characters are opening a lock. *The metal clicks...and releases.* The baton is passed when the next chapter (December 1944) leads with another sound of metal: *Thousand-ton metal shrieks, slowing the train as it pulls into Boston's South Station.*

Then, at the end of Chapter 15, the contemporary protagonist has a sacred, emotional moment of tension. The chapter closes at night with: *And yet she has the sense that somehow she's leaving it behind in the dark.* The next section begins at night, the quiet contemporary ending contrasted by the tension during World War II.

Mirror Theme/Premise in Past & Present

The themes in both the past and present center on forgiveness of one's self and letting go of the past to begin anew. We're not privy to Amanda's premise, but we suspect it went something like this:

Bitterness leads to broken relationships, but grace leads to renewed opportunity and reconciliation.

Stories Collide Near the End

We want to tell you how the past and present stories collide perfectly near the end, but you'll have to read *Whose Waves These Are* to see how it happens. That being said, both the present and past stories bring us back to the lighthouse that Robert has been building. The past story ends when it seems as if there is no hope for completing it. Then the present story begins with a new era of hope and healing for all those who have contributed their stories and stones.

Chapter Five

CATCHING THE WIND
BY MELANIE DOBSON

FOLLOWING IS an analysis of the key elements in ***Catching the Wind***, my fourth time-slip novel, but before I break it down, here is a bit more about the story:

What happened to Brigitte Berthold?

That question has haunted Daniel Knight (Dietmar) since he was thirteen, when he and ten-year-old Brigitte escaped the Gestapo agents who arrested both their parents. They survived a harrowing journey from Germany to England, only to be separated upon their arrival. Daniel vowed to find Brigitte after the war, a promise he has fought to fulfill for more than seventy years.

Now a wealthy old man, Daniel's final hope in finding Brigitte rests with Quenby Vaughn, an American journalist working in London. He believes Quenby's tenacity to find missing people and her personal investment in a related WWII espionage story will help her succeed where previous investigators have failed.

Though Quenby is wrestling her own demons—and wary at the idea of teaming up with Daniel's lawyer, Lucas Hough—the lure of Brigitte's story is too much to resist. Together, Quenby and Lucas delve deep into the past, following a trail of deception, sacrifice, and healing that could change all of their futures.

Multiple Time Periods

The historical plot in *Catching the Wind* begins in 1940 and continues for about seventy years until it merges with the second plotline—a contemporary story set in 2017.

Contemporary Characters Solving Past Mysteries

Daniel Knight has hired many people over the years to search for his childhood friend Brigitte who was taken away after they escaped from Nazi Germany. In his final years of life, Daniel recruits an American reporter to search for Brigitte, and Quenby quickly becomes personally and professionally invested in resolving what happened to this woman.

A ***staccato format*** is the structure for this story, the chapters moving rapidly between past and present. While many time-slip novels don't develop the past-present connection until partway through the story, the main focus of the contemporary characters from the beginning is to solve the mystery of where Brigitte went in 1940 and ultimately what happened after she disappeared.

A Past and Present Protagonist

Quenby is the present-day protagonist, and Daniel Knight (Dietmar) is the main protagonist from the past. Daniel is still alive in the present scenes, but the contemporary story is focused on Quenby's journey. Both Quenby and Daniel experienced loss and abandonment when they were children, and they have both accomplished much as adults.

Different Points of View

The contemporary sections—until near the end—are written from Quenby's third-person perspective while the past scenes are from the third-person perspective of multiple characters including Dietmar/Daniel, Brigitte, Eddie Terrell (the antagonist), and a character named Rosalind who thwarts Eddie's corrupt goals.

Conflict and Character Arc in Both Past & Present Plots

Quenby was wounded deeply as a child after her father died and her mother abandoned her. She has a hard time trusting people and must learn to trust again as she learns what happened to Brigitte and her own mother. Most of the conflict in the contemporary story involves Quenby's personal journey, the search for Brigitte, and the opposition from those modern-day characters who are terrified that Quenby will discover what Brigitte was forced to do during the war.

The past conflict begins in Chapter One with a dramatic escape from the Nazis and then steps into a British spy network. The story spans what happened both during the war and after it, specifically what those men and women involved with spying did to keep their mission secret.

Like the main characters in **Whose Waves These Are**, Quenby and Daniel need each other to complete their separate journeys. Forgiveness is important for both of them—Quenby needs to forgive her mother most of all and Daniel needs to forgive himself. They must work together to complete similar arcs based on very different circumstances.

Bridge to the Past

There are three main bridges that connect the past and present in *Catching the Wind*. Two hand-carved toys—a princess and a knight—make up the first bridge. At the beginning of the book, Daniel keeps the princess that he carved for Brigitte while he gives her the wooden knight, a symbol of his desire to protect her. The second bridge is a journal-of-sorts in the form of letters written on scrap pieces of paper, hidden away in an old tin. These letters begin to tell the story of what happened to Brigitte. The third bridge is a magnolia tree planted in England long ago, a tree that helps lead Quenby to the truth.

Compelling Reason to Solve Mystery NOW

Daniel is an elderly man who has a high regard for faithfulness and friendship. Long ago he promised to find Brigitte, and he has spent a lifetime trying to keep his word. Now he doesn't have much time left to discover the truth, and his final months are dedicated to fulfilling this promise, hoping he can make amends for his failure to her.

In the contemporary plot, Quenby is researching a World War II spy network for an article that she's writing for a news syndicate and her research intersects with Brigitte's story. She is initially motivated as a reporter to uncover the truth about this network, but when someone tries to sabotage her work, she realizes that something bigger than just locating an old friend is at play. After she discovers a personal connection to Brigitte's family, she is highly motivated to solve the mystery as soon as she possibly can.

Backstory Is Front Story

The past story in *Catching the Wind* is foundational to the contemporary plot. It is the backstory for why Daniel is searching for Brigitte and what happened to Quenby's family. Without the past thread, I would have needed to write pages and pages of backstory for their journey to make sense. Through the time-slip structure, I wanted to invite readers to step into the past instead of just inform them about what happened long ago.

TELL in Present Story, SHOW in Past Story

In the present story, Quenby is researching stories about British citizens who supported Nazi Germany during World War II. In her point of view, readers learn about an American woman named Lady Ricker, who married into a wealthy British family. The British government thought Lady Ricker aided the Nazis, but investigators were never able to convict her of this crime.

Readers learn in the contemporary plot that Lady Ricker died in 1953 and they learn the names of her survivors. Then, in the past story, they discover what happened to Lady Ricker and her children. By *telling* key information about this character in the present, I could *show* the emotions of those impacted by her choices in the past scenes.

This technique is a dance—showing in the past, telling in the present, and then showing again in the past until readers have a complete picture of all that occurred. Not repeating unnecessary details, of course, but raising questions and tying together threads along the way without resolving all the conflict until the end.

Foreshadow Past Plot through Present

Bits of foreshadowing are sprinkled throughout the book starting in Chapter Two, the beginning of the contemporary plot. In the present story, readers begin to learn alongside Quenby about the British network of spies and the estate in Kent where Brigitte was first taken. The historical characters, of course, don't know what is coming next, but the readers often do.

Quenby, for example, thinks that Daniel lost Brigitte about seventy years ago, but in Chapter Six, she learns that Brigitte was taken from him. As the historical scenes begin to unfold, the reader discovers exactly how this happened. The foreshadowing from Quenby's discoveries increases the conflict in the story even as it ties the past and present stories together.

Passing the Baton

At the end of Chapter 12, a historical scene, Daniel is shouting for Brigitte while she's being driven away by strangers in a black motorcar, her nose pressed against the back window. He is devastated in this moment, but he is also determined to find her. The baton of the story is then passed ahead seventy years to Quenby who is leaning back on the leather seat of a Range Rover as she and the driver are traveling through London, both of them trying to find out where Brigitte was taken.

Later in the book, another baton is passed from the present story back to the past when a stranger begins to flirt with Quenby. Another woman steps in to stop him and the scene ends. In the next chapter, when the reader slips back into the past, Brigitte is being accosted by a German man. An older woman steps into the scene and redirects the man's attention. It's similar to the scenario with Quenby, but the stakes are much higher for Brigitte.

Mirror Theme/Premise in Past & Present

The past and present themes are centered on faithfulness, forgiveness, and redemption so all the main characters are given an opportunity to be faithful, offer forgiveness, and experience redemption from past wounds.

As I mentioned earlier, the moral premise for *Catching the Wind* is:

Unforgiveness leads to a lifetime of regret, but forgiveness leads to the restoration of relationships.

As a result of each character's choices, whether or not they choose to forgive themselves and others, they either have regret at the end of the story or the restoration of their relationships.

Stories Collide Near the End

The past and present stories begin to collide about three-quarters of the way through *Catching the Wind*. Then a twist fuses together the journey of the heroines from both plot-lines. My stories typically have a surprise ending that ties together most of the main threads. The one thread that I left untied in this story was for the reader's imagination, but the major plot points are resolved when Quenby finally learns where Brigitte went during and after the war.

Chapter Six

Every author who writes time-slip fiction has a unique way of planning, structuring, and communicating their stories. We are super grateful to talented authors Heidi Chiavaroli, Cathy Gohlke, Leslie Gould, Lindsay Harrel, Rachel Hauck, Susan Meissner, and Lisa Wingate for sharing their process and wisdom on how they write split time novels.

Heidi Chiavaroli

AUTHOR BIOGRAPHY

Heidi Chiavaroli is a writer, runner, and grace-clinger who could spend hours exploring places that whisper of historical secrets. Her debut novel, **_Freedom's Ring_**, was a Carol Award winner and a Christy Award finalist, a Romantic Times Top Pick, and a Booklist Top Ten Romance Debut. She makes her home in Massachusetts with her husband and two sons. For more information, visit her website at heidichiavaroli.com.

Heidi Chiavaroli

Why do you write time-split fiction?

When I began writing, I wrote straight historical fiction.
I've always loved history and enjoyed imagining characters
in a long-ago time. And the research! I could geek-out all I
wanted about learning history and now I had a great
excuse!

But after writing four historical manuscripts, one that won a
national contest, I still could not land a contract. It was
about that time I found Susan Meissner and her dual timeline stories. ***A Sound Among the Trees, The Shape of
Mercy, A Fall of Marigolds*** . . . these were like a new
world to me, and I fell in love. I couldn't get enough of
these stories that connected history with the present. In
many ways, this was better than historical fiction because it
added a new layer and meaning to an already wonderful
historical story. A reader could see how contemporary char-

acters are changed and impacted by historical characters. I still get goosebumps thinking about it!

A little unsure of myself, I decided to try my hand at writing this sort of story. I received a contract with my dream agent based on my first time-split story, and a contract with my dream publishing house on my second. It seemed I had found my niche!

Do you prefer to start a novel with a historical or contemporary storyline? Why?

So far, I've always started with the contemporary storyline. I don't think there's a right or a wrong way, but I tend to ground myself by starting with the present day. It gives me perspective on where my contemporary characters are in their journey, where they will end up, and how they will change with the help of my historical characters. More often than not, it will also give me a lens in which to better view my historical story.

I've seen many time-split stories begin with a historical that work well, I just haven't ventured to try it yet!

What is your approach to writing split time?

I always start with how the story is read. Eventually— usually about a quarter of the way through the book—one story will pull me away from the other. (In ***Freedom's Ring*** and ***The Tea Chest***, it was the historical story. In ***The Hidden Side*** and ***The Edge of Mercy***, it was the contemporary one.)

That's when I know what timeline may be the one driving the story. I usually let it take me away! After I'm done, I return to the other timeline. Of course, there are always a lot of edits and finishing touches needed to tie them together, but so far, this method seems to work for me.

What advice do you have for those who want to write split time fiction?

Like any other type of writing, I would say that reading other split time fiction will be helpful. Study how an author tells a successful time-split story.

- What about the connection resonates with you?
- Did the two main characters struggle with a similar issue, even though they are years apart?
- What theme ran throughout the book, tying the timelines together?
- Was there a physical artifact that helped connect the two?

In many ways, time-split stories are like puzzles. If you're a plotter (which I'm not!), you may have an advantage. Try to anticipate and plan how those pieces might come together.

Are your contemporary characters actively seeking a story or mystery from the past? Or will the historical characters impact them in a more unexpected way?

If you are a pantser (plotting a story by the seat of your pants) then simply write and trust your instincts. You can always stop and brainstorm and redirect the story if you feel the characters are just not working with you!

Cathy Gohlke

AUTHOR BIOGRAPHY

Cathy Gohlke is the three-time Christy Award-winning author of critically acclaimed novels including her split time novel, ***Secrets She Kept***, which was the winner of the Christy, 2016 Carol and INSPY Awards. When not traveling to historic sites for research, she, her husband, and their dog, Reilly, divide their time between Northern Virginia and the Jersey Shore, enjoying time with their grown children and grandchildren. For more information, visit her website at cathygohlke.com.

Cathy Gohlke

Since you've mainly written other novels that are single timeline, why did you decide to write a dual timeline one?

Writing **Secrets She Kept** was a special case for me—a wrestling with questions close to my heart. We can repent and receive forgiveness for our sins, but how do we address the sins of our parents or grandparents—sins and shame that have shaped or still affect our lives and/or the lives of others? Can we atone for things they've done? Is there a way to make it right? What if the wrongs committed against others are so heinous that they can't be undone? Can they be forgiven by those who suffered terrible loss? Can we forgive our family?

Because these questions involve both what happened in the past and how we deal with the present, I needed to tell both sides of the story, really get into the heads of those living with the crimes of the past and those dealing with the fallout in more recent times. I also needed to show the perpetrators' side of the story through the political and social lens of their time, twisted though that was.

Writing a dual timeline was the only way I knew to fully explore all sides of the characters and the relevant questions.

What was the experience like writing a dual time vs a single timeline?

Surprising to me, writing a dual timeline was thrilling and easier for me than I'd expected. I loved being able to explore current issues from the perspective of both the past and present—limiting myself to the points of view and understanding that each character would have encountered and experienced in their time, then compare, contrast, and weave those together.

I loved exploring how the decisions of parents shape their children and grandchildren, scrutinizing the fallout from past decisions in multiple generations. It made me keenly aware of how our decisions affect others, especially our children and grandchildren.

Writing a dual timeline was a new and growing experience for me, so I think that any difficulties I encountered were lost in the joy and thrill of the adventure. This book was in many ways the easiest book I've ever written. I think that is because I'd wondered about the questions it raises for many years so the issues were very clear in my mind.

I was also able to interview a number of Holocaust survivors, the children of their generation, and Germans who'd experienced the war—military and civilian. Their accounts, woven into fiction, made the text come alive. I'd not been able to find a way to tell this story until I settled on writing a dual timeline. That made exploring past tragedies and their generational repercussions possible.

What is your approach to writing split time?

In writing **Secrets She Kept** I wrote one storyline at a time, then wove them both together. At first, I tried writing alternating chapters, but found it too confusing to jump from one time period to another—to get in my modern character's head then jump into the past. For me, that was like writing two different books at once. I just couldn't seem to do it and it felt like work and agony. Writing is joy for me, so when I find it feels like work I know I need to stand back and ask why, regroup, and begin again.

When I allowed myself to stay in one storyline at a time, the words flowed. I became so caught up in each character and their dilemmas that I really felt I was those characters. It was exhilarating.

Once each storyline neared completion, I began weaving the two together, tweaking to reveal the story of the past only as the more modern character came to a point in her journey that it was needed and would have the most impact. The last few chapters were written after that weaving, helping me bring the story to a satisfying conclusion.

What advice do you have for those who want to write split time fiction?

Focus on a central question or issue that links the two time periods. *What is the connection between the two—the thing that weaves the two stories together?* This is the common thread. This thread will create a roadmap—a pathway along which your chosen theme will reveal itself through your characters' experiences and their reactions to those experiences.

Fully research and explore both time periods—the political, social, and religious issues, the thinking, reasoning, and moral lens of the time periods in which you set your story, as well as details of daily life needed for any story. Immerse yourself in the difficulties and questions your characters must face given what you learn of their time period.

Create unique inner voices as well as appropriate dialect in dialogue for your characters, making certain those voices reflect the two different time periods. Weave both stories in a way that reveals what must be known only as needed. This approach maintains suspense and will lead readers to the "aha!" moment.

Leslie Gould

Leslie Gould is the bestselling and Christy Award-winning author of over thirty novels including an Amish split time series, **The Sisters of Lancaster County**, and split time series, **Cousins of the Dove**, co-written with Mindy Starns Clark. Leslie loves traveling, research, Shakespeare's plays, and church history. She and her husband live in Portland, Oregon, and are the parents of four children. For more information, visit her website at lesliegould.com.

Leslie Gould

Why do you write time-split fiction?

In *Requiem for a Nun*, William Faulkner wrote, "The past is never dead. It's not even the past." The older I grow, the more I agree with the quote. As a child, I loved Madeleine L'Engle's novel *A Wrinkle in Time* and the concept of time and dimensionality. The same is true with the past. It's only a second away in our memory, and not only our own past but also the pasts of our parents, grandparents, and great-grandparents—as long as those stories have been shared.

Why do I write time-split fiction? Because, besides exploring the past and its impact on my own family, I also want to do that in other "families" and "worlds" too, worlds where I can create all of the unknown details I can't determine for sure in real life. So far, I've written about or am currently writing split time fiction that includes seventeenth century France, eighteenth century Williamsburg, the Revolutionary War, the Indian removal period of the nineteenth century, the

Underground Railroad, the American Civil War, the Chicago Fire of 1871, the War to End All Wars, and World War Two—and I've loved every minute of it!

Do you prefer to start a novel with a historical or contemporary storyline? Why?

So far, all but one of the novels I've written have started with the contemporary story. The other one, ***My Brother's Crown***, co-written with Mindy Starns Clark, started with a very brief, historical prologue to set up that thread—but the historical main character wasn't introduced until after the contemporary main character was.

I'm not opposed to starting a novel with the historical character though, if that works best for the novel! But so far, in each of my novels, the main contemporary character learns something from the historical story that helps her solve a mystery or make an important decision in her own life. She's the one searching for an answer, so it makes sense to start the novel with her.

What first drew you to read this genre? And then to write it?

I majored in history in my undergrad studies but started out writing contemporary fiction. Once I began reading split time novels, I was hooked! It was the best of two worlds. I find it both challenging and super rewarding!

What is your approach to writing split time?

I really mix it up as far as my approach to writing split time fiction and have done it differently with nearly each novel that I've written. Sometimes I'll write it chapter by chapter, jumping back and forth from the contemporary to the historical stories.

Other times I've written the entire contemporary story first and then the historical thread. Other times I've written the first few chapters of the contemporary story, then all of the historical story, and then I've gone back and finished the contemporary story.

How do I choose which approach I use? I do whichever one inspires me to write the fastest because I'm always on deadline. Mixing it up and following my intuition for each story keeps things fresh for me. However, I do always write a long outline—fifteen pages or so before I start the actual writing—that includes a paragraph for each scene in the story. That keeps my writing moving along and keeps me on target as far as the plot, characters, and structure of the story.

What advice do you have for those who want to write split time fiction?

First, read split time fiction! See how other authors do it. Examine each of the two (or more) points of view, how the novel is structured, and what connects the two (or more) threads. Next, plan to spend a good chunk of time planning out your story.

Figure out what the connection is between the past and the

present in your story. *Is your contemporary character solving a mystery with the information that the past character "reveals"? Will your contemporary character be inspired to do the right thing or make a hard decision based on what she learns from the historical character?*

Be clear what the story questions are for both of your main characters and then map the two threads out in detail. Journal from your characters' points of view if that helps. Think through what artifacts and metaphors can span the two stories and help connect them. Think through the minor characters in each thread and how you can connect them too. Brainstorm with a writer friend if possible. Plan to spend double the time planning a split time novel as you would a regular one.

Lindsay Harrel

AUTHOR BIOGRAPHY

Lindsay Harrel is a lifelong book nerd with a B.A. in journalism and an M.A. in English. She has held a variety of jobs and now juggles stay-at-home mommyhood with working freelance jobs, teaching college English courses online, and—of course—writing novels, including her split time novel, ***The Secrets of Paper and Ink***. She lives in Arizona with her young family and two golden retrievers in serious need of training. For more information, visit her website at lindsayharrel.com.

Since you've mainly written other novels that are single timeline, why did you decide to write a dual timeline one?

Honestly, I had just read **Before We Were Yours** by Lisa Wingate and was super inspired by that book. I'd also just read a handful of historical novels and really wanted to write something different than I'd written before.

I love both the Regency and Victorian eras and knew my next book would be set in England. So I scrapped the straight contemporary plot I had started writing (I'd written about a quarter of the book already) and completely replotted it with a historical timeline.

What was the experience like writing a dual time vs a single timeline?

I wouldn't necessarily say it was MORE difficult, but it was different. In many ways, the story just spilled out of me—so I think that some books are just easier to write than others depending on the content and the current circumstances of your life. However, I will say that new challenges included weaving the past and present storylines together and checking all the historical details. I used an etymology dictionary online to make sure I wasn't using a word that hadn't come into fashion yet and delved deep into research books on the time period. Of course, you still have to do lots of research even in writing a single timeline story.

What is your approach to writing split time?

For the one split-time story I've written so far, I found it easiest to write the entire historical timeline first and then figure out where those scenes fit within the contemporary one.

What advice do you have for those who want to write split time fiction?

Don't be intimidated! I was nervous to write a new kind of story but found that it came together much more easily than I would have anticipated. Also, I'd say some planning/plotting might be necessary. Of course, I'm a plotter anyway. The idea of pantsing a story that requires weaving together two timelines makes me shudder!

Rachel Hauck

AUTHOR BIOGRAPHY

Rachel Hauck is a *New York Times, USA Today,* and *Wall Street Journal* bestselling author. She is a Christy Award winner and a double RITA finalist. Her split time novel **The Wedding Dress** was named Inspirational Novel of the Year by Romantic Times Book Club. She is also the recipient of RT's Career Achievement Award, and her book, **Once Upon A Prince**, was made into an original Hallmark movie.

A graduate of Ohio State University with a degree in Journalism and a former sorority girl, Rachel and her husband live in central Florida. She is a huge Buckeyes football fan. For more information, visit her website at www.rachelhauck.com.

Rachel Hauck

Why do you write time-split fiction?

For me it started as a love for the style, which I discovered in Susan Meissner's **Shape of Mercy**. When I started **The Wedding Dress**, I knew the historical story had to be told along with the contemporary story. I love the idea of "looking into the past" to see the lives and decisions of our ancestors.

Do you prefer to start a novel with a historical or contemporary storyline? Why?

I think for split time authors you have to start with both. For me they come at the same time. With split time, there's usually an object or event that anchors the story. So I'd really say start with the lynchpin that launches both stories. What is that "thing" that existed in the past yet has impact in the present?

What is your approach to writing split time?

I write the historical and contemporary pieces together. If I start in the past, then the next scene is in the present. If I start in the present, the next scene is in the past. Since I usually have four point-of-view characters, I try to establish the heroines first with a couple of scenes. Then I introduce the heroes. Split time "romance" leans more toward contemporary fiction with the heroines being the predominant story tellers but you can have your heroes be just as dynamic.

What advice do you have for those who want to write split time fiction?

Have a passion for it. Don't write it because it's the "latest" thing. Know that you have a strong story in the past as well as the present. Develop all the characters to the fullest.

Each point of view character must have all the elements of a great protagonist: a problem, obstacles, wants, goals, epiphany, black moment, overcoming, and happy ending. You can't shortchange any of the characters. Resign yourself to the idea the book will be at least 90,000 to 100,000 words to do the characters and the ending justice. After telling the two stories, you must tie them together. Study other split time authors and then go for it.

Susan Meissner

AUTHOR BIOGRAPHY

Susan Meissner is the *USA Today* bestselling author of historical fiction with more than half a million books in print in fifteen languages. Her novels include ***The Last Year of the War***, a Library Reads and Real Simple top pick; ***As Bright as Heaven***, which received a starred review from Library Journal; ***Secrets of a Charmed Life***, a 2015 Goodreads Choice award finalist; and ***A Fall of Marigolds***, named to Booklist's Top Ten women's fiction titles for 2014. She is also a RITA finalist and Christy Award and Carol Award winner. A California native, she is also a writing workshop volunteer for Words Alive, a San Diego nonprofit dedicated to helping at-risk youth foster a love for reading and writing. For more information, visit her website at www.susanmeissner.com.

Why do you write time-split fiction?

I don't always write split-time fiction, but when I do, it's always because the story just called for it, and I was happy to oblige. For me, split time works best when the story in the past meshes with the story in the present in a way that results in organic relevance. The two narratives need to matter to each other such that the past somehow affects change (either good or bad) when it collides with the story in the present.

Do you prefer to start a novel with a historical or contemporary storyline? Why?

I am almost always inspired first by a historical context of some kind, but I don't always start with it. I try to make all my decisions for the story's good, not my own.

My preferences always have to be second to the story's needs. I don't think of myself as a slave to the story, though. I am still the master of the narrative; I just choose to make decisions on what is best for the story, not what is easiest or best or preferred by me.

What first drew you to read and write this genre?

I read **The Thirteenth Tale** in 2006 by Diane Setterfield and loved it. I was enamored by the story's dual time periods construction—so much so that I wrote my first split time periods book, **The Shape of Mercy**, the next year. It released at a time when that kind of book was relatively new. I loved using the past (by telling it) to speak not just to my present-day character, but also the present-day reader.

What is your approach to writing split time?

Most of my dual storylines have been written simultaneously since I learn so much about the main characters by actually writing their story. It's usually easier to see how the two main characters, separated by time, are distinct and/or similar if I write them at the same time. Often by the halfway mark, I will spend more time on one storyline than the other as the momentum and tension builds.

What advice do you have for those who want to write split time fiction?

I think it's always wise to think about the effectiveness of the split-time narrative on the story you want to tell. I can usually tell when an author feels nudged by the market to write split-time and then imposes that template on a story that would've perhaps stood fine with a solo time stamp. Or might have been better.

93

Remember, the story will tell you what it wants. Listen to it.

Lisa Wingate

AUTHOR BIOGRAPHY

Lisa Wingate is the author of the #1 *New York Times* bestseller **Before We Were Yours**, which remained on the bestseller list for fifty-four weeks in hardcover and has sold over 2 million copies. She has penned over thirty novels and co-authored a nonfiction book, *Before and After,* with Judy Christie. Her award-winning works have been selected for state and community One Book reads throughout the country, have been published in over forty languages, and have appeared on bestseller lists worldwide. Booklist summed up her work by saying, "Lisa Wingate is, quite simply, a master storyteller." She lives with her husband in North Texas. For more information, visit her website at www.lisawingate.com.

Why do you write time-split fiction?

I love working in dual time frames, telling a historical tale
interlaced with a contemporary one. There's something
about the juxtaposition of a modern life and a life (real or
fictional) of long ago that lends reality to both tales.

What is your approach to writing split time?

I'm a completely linear writer—I write the book just as the
reader will eventually read it, rather than writing the
contemporary and historical stories separately and then
threading them together. I think that's partly because I'm
more of a discover-as-I-go writer than an intense pre-
plotter.

What advice do you have for those who want to write split time fiction?

There are a few tricks that help intertwined dual timeframe narratives to interact in meaningful ways:

Even though you're telling two stories, one narrator's story will control the pace and drive of the story. Typically, that's the present-day narrator, who is discovering or in some way mirroring the life of the historical character.

It's helpful to employ a physical connection between the characters—an object, a place, a written record like letters in a prayer box. In my novel, ***The Story Keeper***, the connection between a modern-day editor and a Melungeon girl in turn-of-the-century Appalachia is an old partial manuscript that lands unexpectedly on an editor's desk. Her search for the rest of the manuscript takes her on a journey back to the Blue Ridge.

One story must significantly affect the other. Perhaps the modern character is learning from the story of the historical character. Perhaps he or she is living through events and emotional changes that mirror those of the historical character. Perhaps the modern character is solving an age-old mystery, clearing the name of the historical character (in ***Wildwood Creek***, modern-day Allie is clearing the name of historical Bonnie Rose, who stood accused of mass murder).

Perhaps the modern character is making her counterpart's place in history known to the world. Perhaps the characters are distantly or closely related, and the quest is an issue of family, identity, or ancestry, as when Benny's students discover their heritage in Hannie's Reconstruction Era sojourn in ***The Book of Lost Friends***.

The possibilities are many with dual timeframe stories. I never know exactly where each story will lead, but ultimately the journey of discovery is a thrilling ride!

AUTHOR INTERVIEW

Why do you write time-split fiction?

I'm the reader who loves epilogues. I want to know what happens after the official story is over. The time-slip genre gives me the opportunity as a writer to communicate the story after the story. I can write, for example, about how something that happened during World War II continues to impact people today.

In **Shadows of Ladenbrooke Manor**, my hero discusses the reality of 20/20 hindsight for his own situation and family. "What we discover," he writes after a heartbreaking revelation, "changes how we view the past, and then we can choose—quite deliberately—to change our future."

The medium of split time fiction demonstrates beautifully the threads, both good and bad, that connect generations. It shows how discovering our character's history can heal current wounds. I love the mystery and romance of this genre. The secrets revealed and battles won. Most of all, I love the hope that can prevail after heartbreak. The possibilities of redemption at the very end.

Do you prefer to start a novel with a historical or contemporary storyline? Why?

Every novel is different, but usually I start in the historical setting because my plots revolve around a mystery from the past. Then I ask my contemporary characters why it's urgent for them to discover what happened decades ago. Their answer (yes, I talk *and* listen to my characters!) will determine how my present-day hero and heroine will move the story forward.

Most of us who write split time seem to lean naturally toward a focus on either the contemporary or historical plotline. The same year, for example, that ***Chateau of Secrets*** won the Carol Award for Historical Fiction, Lisa Wingate's marvelous dual timeline novel ***The Story Keeper*** received the Carol for Contemporary Fiction.

This is one of the many things I love about our emerging genre—time-slip writers have very different ways of weaving together a story. No two novels are structured exactly alike.

What is your approach to writing split time?

I brainstorm pieces of the present and past timelines individually, then I weave the story together in my manuscript to reveal the right information at the right time. I am more of a seat-of-the-pants creator than a planner, although I've learned from experience that I need a general roadmap for which direction I'm headed before I set out. I still do a lot of mental meandering along my journey. Sometimes I even end up close to my intended destination.

My first draft is *very* messy. I have to rewrite multiple times to connect and clean up all the pieces, much more editing than I've ever had to do in straight historical or contemporary fiction. It's a huge challenge . . . and tons of fun.

What advice do you have for those who want to write split time fiction?

Get your story poured out onto paper first. Then you can rearrange and polish and tweak until it's ready for publication. Anne Lamott says:

> "Perfectionism is the voice of the oppressor, the enemy of the people. It will keep you cramped and insane your whole life, and it is the main obstacle between you and a 'bad' first draft . . ."

Time-slip fiction is difficult to write, but it's also very rewarding. If you have a story burning inside you, please write, edit, and then release it so readers can enjoy the journey with you.

Chapter Seven

NOTEBOOKS, journals, binders, Scrivener, or a mass of notes pinned to a giant corkboard—numerous ways exist to plot and brainstorm your next split time novel. The process of trying to figure out what works for you can be an extremely overwhelming one.

Morgan Tarpley Smith

I am speaking from experience. I've tried all of the above options, and I think I've finally narrowed down what works for me (a combo of a notebook and binder).

The question is:
what do you think will work for you?

WHEN I first set out to write a time-slip novel years ago I had no idea where to begin, so I turned to blog posts and the websites of my favorite split time authors for advice.

Kate Morton

Australian author Kate Morton's split time novels have sold millions of copies and been translated into many languages. She's one of my all-time favorite authors, so, of course, I had to pay attention to how she crafts such complex and unique twists and turns in her stories.

In an interview with Historical Novels Review, Morton explains how she uses notebooks/journals in her writing process.

> "I am absolutely a notebook person. To imagine being without one fills me with dread . . . By the time I finish writing a novel, I've usually gathered around ten notebooks of story ideas, random images, plot schematics, scene details, graphs, snatches of overheard conversation. . . you name it, it's in there. Scribbled, crossed-out, connected with arrows, stapled in on top of other bits and pieces. Quite a mess, but a somehow lovely one. I'm a visual person and to see them sketched out in my notebook helps me to clarify my thoughts and pin down my ideas. Also, the pen in hand forces me to focus."

I love notebooks and journals and paper too! Like Morton I think the pen in hand and the blank pages of a journal or notebook peering back at me is a fantastic way to dive into a story. It's one of my main go-to brainstorming methods where I can scribble and dream of any direction that the story might go.

Morton also says when she gets stuck in her writing, she'll go to a cozy corner of a coffee shop, notebook in hand, and start writing as fast and furious as she can until the ideas start flowing again. Then she's back deep into the world of her novel.

Susanna Kearsley

Another of my favorite split time authors is *New York Times* best-selling Canadian novelist Susanna Kearsley. I was thrilled to speak with Kearsley recently at a reader's event and discuss how she organizes her research for novels.

She directed me to **Guide to Fiction Writing** by Phyllis A. Whitney, the book that helped her when she first started writing. Whitney was a prolific author of romantic suspense novels with a career that spanned over sixty years. She published this book on writing in the 1980s, but it is still very relevant today, especially when it comes to her notebook system, which she cited for keeping her organized and helping her avoid writer's block.

Kearsley developed this system into one of her own using a three-ring binder with different sections for Research, Timeline/Chronology, Things to Check, Characters, Setting and more. As Kearsley read through her primary sources and other research materials, she recorded her ideas in the binder and referenced her notes as she wrote. Currently, she saves research and documents on her computer and also has physical copies of research organized in a folder.

Other authors I know use the Evernote app to digitally

organize their research or other programs such as Scrivener. I put my own spin on a combination of Morton and Kearsley's methods by using a brainstorming notebook and a small binder for plotting and outlining as I research and jot down ideas.

Melanie Dobson

I organize all of my historical and contemporary research under folders in Scrivener. I also keep detailed biographies of my main characters and setting descriptions in a Scrivener binder.

My actual writing is not nearly as organized as the research because my creativity does not conform well to computer folders and files. When it's time for me to actively brainstorm, I love pouring ideas into a notebook, the pen slowing down my racing mind. If I don't have my notebook, I turn to the Notes app on my phone or scrap paper in the car, scribbling down ideas while waiting for my girls to finish their activities. Some of my best story twists, I think, have been recorded on random bits of paper.

Even though I've longed for the ability to plot and outline an entire novel like Morgan and other writer friends, I've learned that too much outlining stifles my creative process. So, I organize as I write, transferring my ideas into Scrivener and writing in Microsoft Word.

Every morning I edit what I wrote the prior day before pouring new words onto my screen. Then, after I complete a chapter, I revise my Scrivener outline to help keep track of the information that I'm revealing in my time-slip threads. This software separation between my manuscript and organization/ideas is good for my messy mind.

Chapter Eight

HOPEFULLY, you have a plethora of ideas running through your mind now to begin a new manuscript or guidelines to rewrite and tweak an existing time-slip story.

So, what to do now?

First of all, reread one of your favorite split time novels and use the following exercise to do your own Novel Analysis. Get to the heart of why you love that particular story. *Is it the structure or a character's point of view? The setting or description? Do you prefer its contemporary or historical storyline and why?*

Now, analyze your own novel idea or your existing manuscript and see how it measures up. Locate weaknesses or holes in your plot and brainstorm ways to strengthen or fix them.

Check out the resources we have mentioned in this book, whether it be about the craft of fiction writing or **splittimefiction.com** for a library of time-slip books.

And I (Morgan) want to extend a personal invitation for

you to check out my Facebook group for readers of time-slip fiction, ***A Split in Time***, where we chat about all things split time. As its companion, I created ***Split Time Fiction That Travels***, a Goodreads group that contains an ever-growing comprehensive list of split time novels organized by labels such as setting, book release year, historical events, and time periods.

At the heart of split time is just that—*heart*—and its visceral connection to the past, where there is so much yet to absorb and learn from those who have gone before us. Through writing this genre we are not only preserving the past but making history come alive in some form to our readers, opening their minds and hearts to important and relevant truths within the silvery strands of time.

We hope you join us on this journey!

Additional Material

CHECKLISTS, WORKSHEETS, AND EXERCISES

Review Checklist

COMMON MISTAKES IN SPLIT TIME FICTION

1. Repeating information in past and present plots
2. A missing token or symbol that bridges the past to the present
3. Contemporary characters who don't have a connection to the historical plot
4. Contradicting a prior chapter or revealing something not yet ready to be revealed in the contemporary storyline
5. Imbalance between past and present plots
6. An extensive cast without differentiating the characters
7. Neglecting an urgent reason for the contemporary characters to act now
8. Forgetting to establish a clear internal journey for the past and present protagonists so they both have to choose between good and evil in their lives
9. Rough transitions between past and present

10. Discord between the concluding timelines
11. No surprise at the end

Novel Analysis

Before you begin working on your time-slip story, we recommend that you read one of your favorite split time novels (one that really inspires you) and analyze it based on the information in this book, getting to the heart of why you love this particular novel.

Below are a few questions to get you started:

Multiple Time Periods

How many storylines does the novel contain (two or more?)

What is the time period of the storylines (all historical, all contemporary, combination of contemporary and historical)?

Is it a Staccato, Sandwich or Sectional story?

Contemporary Characters Solving Past Mysteries

What is the contemporary protagonist highly motivated to find out about the past?

Is there an unsolved mystery surrounding a murder, a missing person, or a mysterious object (or a combination of several mysteries) for the contemporary character to solve?

A Past and Present Protagonist

What do the protagonists want and intently pursue throughout the novel? What are the characters' wants and goals that readers deeply care about?

Different Points of View

What point of view is used for your protagonists (both third person, both first person, or a combo of first and third person)?

Conflict and Character Arc in Both Past & Present Plots

How will the contemporary character go in a whole new direction and be forever changed externally and internally by her discovery about the past?

Bridge to the Past

What is the token or symbol (bridge to the past) that ties together the past and present storylines?

Compelling Reason to Solve Mystery NOW

Why does the mystery need to be solved now for the contemporary characters? What has happened to make this an urgent matter to resolve?

What is the inciting incident and point of no return for each protagonist?

Backstory is Front Story

Does the novel begin with a past or present storyline?

Why is the backstory necessary for the plot to be complete?

TELL in Present Story, SHOW in Past Story

What time period is featured in the historical storyline? Is it a well-known one?

Does the contemporary protagonist already have some information about the historical period or past characters?

Foreshadow Past Plot through Present

How does the contemporary character's research and knowledge foreshadow pieces of the plot in the past storyline?

Passing the Baton

Was the "pass the baton" technique used in the novel?

What are some ways the author transitioned between storylines?

Mirror Theme/Premise in Past & Present

What is the main theme (grief, forgiveness, identity, etc.) for the story?

Is there a moral premise?

If so, how would you define it?

*(NEGATIVE CHOICE)*___________________

*leads to (VICE)*________________,

*but (POSITIVE CHOICE)*________________

*leads to (VIRTUE)*________________.

What dilemmas do the protagonists and antagonists both face based on this vice and virtue?

Stories Collide Near the End

How do the protagonists wrestle with the moral premise or story theme a final time?

How do the storylines intersect with a huge collision?

Which threads and major plot points does the author use to stitch up the novel near the end?

In what way or ways does the historical story change the contemporary protagonist's life?

Your Novel Analysis

WORKSHEET #2

Now, analyze your own novel idea or your existing manuscript and see how it measures up to the Novel Analysis you did while reading that favorite novel.

Multiple Time Periods

How many storylines does your novel contain (two or more?)

What is the time period of the storylines (all historical, all contemporary, combination of contemporary and historical)?

Is it a Staccato, Sandwich or Sectional story?

Contemporary Characters Solving Past Mysteries

What is the contemporary protagonist highly motivated to find out about the past?

Is there an unsolved mystery surrounding a murder, a missing person, or a mysterious object (or a combination of several mysteries) for the contemporary character to solve?

A Past and Present Protagonist

What do your protagonists want and intently pursue throughout the novel? What are your characters' wants and goals that readers deeply care about?

Different Points of View

What point of view is used for your protagonists (both third person, both first person, or a combo of first and third person)?

Conflict and Character Arc in Both Past & Present Plots

How will your contemporary character go in a whole new direction and be forever changed externally and internally by her discovery about the past?

Bridge to the Past

What is the token or symbol (bridge to the past) that ties together the past and present storylines?

Compelling Reason to Solve Mystery NOW

Why does the mystery need to be solved now for the contemporary characters? What has happened to make this an urgent matter to resolve?

What is the inciting incident and point of no return for each protagonist?

Backstory is Front Story

Does your novel begin with a past or present storyline?

Why is the backstory necessary for the plot to be complete?

TELL in Present Story, SHOW in Past Story

What time period is featured in your historical storyline? Is it a well-known one?

Does your contemporary protagonist already have some information about the historical period or past characters?

Foreshadow Past Plot through Present

How does the contemporary character's research and knowledge foreshadow pieces of the plot in the past storyline?

Passing the Baton

Will the "pass the baton" technique be used in your novel?

What are some ways you can transition between the storylines?

Mirror Theme/Premise in Past & Present

What is the main theme (grief, forgiveness, identity, etc.) for your story?

Is there a moral premise?

If so, how would you define it?

    *(NEGATIVE CHOICE)*_________________

    *leads to (VICE)*_______________,

    *but (POSITIVE CHOICE)*_______________

    *leads to (VIRTUE)*_______________.

What dilemmas will your protagonists and antagonists both face based on this vice and virtue?

Stories Collide Near the End

How do your protagonists wrestle with the moral premise or story theme a final time?

How do your storylines intersect with a huge collision?

Which threads and major plot points will you use to stitch up the novel near the end?

In what way or ways does your historical story change the contemporary protagonist's life?

Jump-Start Your Split Time Novel

WORKSHEET #3

Even those who prefer writing as a *pantser* should do a little planning before launching into your split time novel.

Here are some basic questions to jump-start your story:

Number of storylines in your book?

What is the time period of the storylines? (all historical, all contemporary, combination of contemporary and historical)

Present Timeline

Settings:

Year:

Who is the Protagonist?

Protagonist Point of View:

What is Her/His Primary Goal?

What is Keeping the Protagonist from Obtaining Her/His Goal?

Past Timeline

Settings:

Year:

Who is the Protagonist?

Protagonist Point of View?

What is Her/His Primary Goal?

What is Keeping the Protagonist from Obtaining Her/His Goal?

Bridge to the Past (event, objects, etc.)?

Story Structure (Staccato, Sectional, or Sandwich)?

Story Begins with the Present or Past?

Review Checklist

ADVANCED QUESTIONS FOR YOUR STORY

1. Why does your story have to be told through split time?
2. Will your contemporary protagonist already know some information about the past?
3. What is the inciting incident and point of no return for each protagonist?
4. Why is your contemporary protagonist highly motivated to find out what happened in the past?
5. How will the contemporary character be forever changed externally and internally by her discovery?
6. Which twist(s) will surprise your reader?
7. How will you stitch up the threads of your story in the end?

Recommended Resources

Writing Books

- ***The 38 Most Common Fiction Writing Mistakes*** by Jack M. Bickham
- ***45 Master Characters*** by Victoria Lynn Schmidt
- ***Between the Lines*** by Jessica Page Morrell
- ***The Forest for the Trees*** by Betsy Lerner
- ***Guide to Fiction Writing*** by Phyllis A. Whitney
- ***How to Grow a Novel*** by Sol Stein
- ***The Moral Premise: Harnessing Virtue & Vice for Box Office Success*** by Stanley Williams
- ***Plot & Structure*** by James Scott Bell
- ***Write Your Novel from the Middle*** by James Scott Bell

- ***Writing the Breakout Novel*** by Donald Maass

Online Resources

- **splittimefiction.com**
- **morgantarpleysmith.com**
- **A Split in Time Fiction Facebook Group**
- **Split Time Fiction that Travels Goodreads Group**
- **advancedfictionwriting.com e-zine**
- ***Great Courses: How to Write Best-Selling Fiction*** by James Scott Bell, thegreatcourses.com/courses/how-to-write-best-selling-fiction.html
- ***The Creative Penn*** podcast, thecreativepenn.com/podcasts/
- ***Novel Marketing*** podcast , authormedia.com/novel-marketing/

Acknowledgments

We are incredibly thankful for the many people who inspired and helped us through the writing of this book. Thank you to our first readers who assisted us with the editing and gave us invaluable input: Sandra Byrd, Julie McDonald Zander, Tracie Heskett, and Carole Lehr Johnson. You are all amazing writers and friends!

A special thank you to Heidi Chiavaroli, Cathy Gohlke, Leslie Gould, Lindsay Harrel, Rachel Hauck, Susan Meissner, and Lisa Wingate for sharing your journey and many years of writing wisdom with us. To Victoria Davies at VC Book Covers for our cover design. And thank you again to Amanda Dykes for allowing us to analyze your beautiful novel.

MORGAN'S NOTE

First of all, I would like to thank Melanie for taking the chance to co-author a book with someone she didn't know. It has been such a blessing to work with you. I cherish our friendship. I would like to thank my husband, Steven, for always supporting my writing endeavors; my mother, Mellanie, for being my forever #1 writing fan and Carole Lehr Johnson, the best writing partner and dearest friend, who introduced me to this beautiful writing style.

I would also like to thank my huge circle of family and friends who are ever supportive and encouraging. I appreciate you all. And I would like to thank God for always directing me on new and exciting paths even when I feel inadequate and unworthy. He is the creative spark within this writer.

MELANIE'S NOTE

Morgan—it has been such a joy to work with you on this! Thank you for your enthusiasm and wisdom and for helping me grow. I've loved everything about our process and so appreciate all of your direction to create the perfect-for-us cover.

Thank you to Natasha Kern for encouraging me to pursue my dream of writing time-slip fiction. To Jon, Karlyn, and Kiki—thank you for always cheering me on.

And thank you, most of all, to the Master Creator for His many gifts to all of us.

About the Author

MELANIE DOBSON

Writing fiction is Melanie Dobson's excuse to explore abandoned houses, travel to unique places, and spend hours reading old journals and books. The award-winning author of more than twenty novels, Melanie enjoys stitching together both time-slip and historical fiction including *Catching the*  *Wind, Hidden Among the Stars*, and *Memories of Glass*. Melanie's novels have won four Carol Awards, the Audie Award, and the ForeWord Book of the Year. The Dobson family resides in the Pacific Northwest where she enjoys hiking, teaching, playing games with her husband and girls, and loving on kids in their community.

Find more information about her journey here:

www.melaniedobson.com
facebook.com/MelanieDobsonFiction
instagram.com/melbdobson

About the Author

MORGAN TARPLEY SMITH

Morgan Tarpley Smith is an award-winning newspaper reporter and photographer in Louisiana. She writes split time fiction and is the founder of *A Split in Time Fiction Group* on Facebook and the *Split Time Fiction that Travels Group* on Goodreads. Besides writing and traveling to over a dozen countries, her interests include hanging out at coffee shops, listening to records, and researching genealogy. She loves going on adventures with her family.

For more information, visit:

www.morgantarpleysmith.com
facebook.com/MorganTarpleySmith
instagram.com/writerchic86

www.ingramcontent.com/pod-product-compliance
Lightning Source LLC
Chambersburg PA
CBHW072003210726
48292CB00021B/2810